For schoolteachers everywhere
—J.M.

For Kelsey Holinka
—W.W.

Text copyright © 2012 by Jean Marzollo.
"Arts & Crafts" from *I Spy: A Book of Picture Riddles* © 1992 by Walter Wick; "Circus Band" from *I Spy Fun House* © 1993 by Walter Wick; "Chain Reaction" from *I Spy Mystery* © 1993 by Walter Wick; "1, 2, 3…," "A Is for…," "Chalkboard Fun," "Mapping," and "Stegosaurus" from *I Spy School Days* © 1995 by Walter Wick; "The Rainbow Express" from *I Spy Fantasy* © 1994 by Walter Wick; "View from Duck Pond Inn" from *I Spy Treasure Hunt* © 1999 by Walter Wick.

Library of Congress Cataloging-in-Publication Data is available.

ISBN 978-0-545-40281-1

10 9 8 7   15 16

Printed in the U.S.A. 40 • First printing, July 2012

I SPY
SCHOOL

Riddles by Jean Marzollo
Photographs by Walter Wick

SCHOLASTIC INC.

I spy

a school bus,

 a bright blue van,

a yellow speedboat,

 and a policeman.

I spy

scissors,

 a small red rose,

a roll of tape,

 and a puppy's black nose.

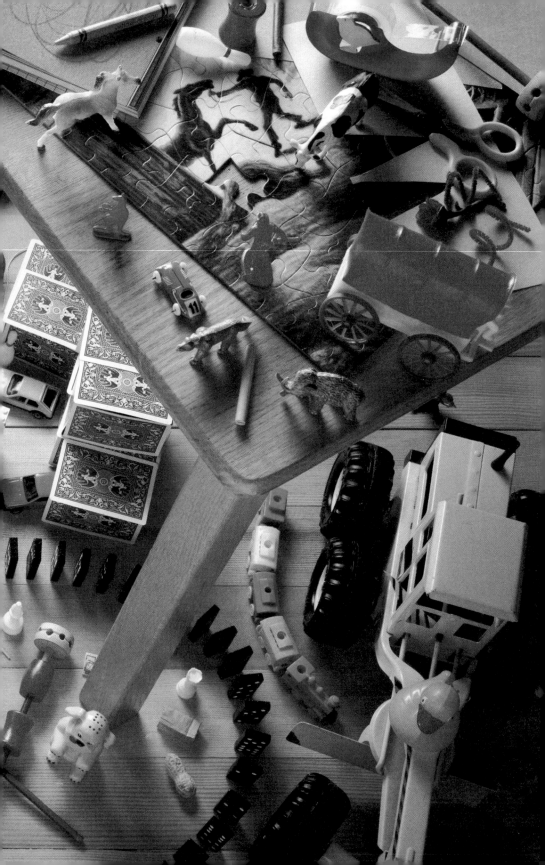

I spy

 a whistle,

a hammer,

 a ship,

a piece of chalk,

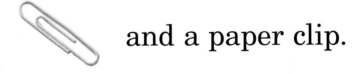 and a paper clip.

I spy

 a ladybug,

a silver key,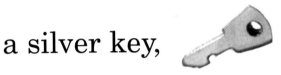

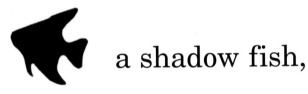 a shadow fish,

an R, **R**

E and an E.

I spy

a ruler,

 an egg that's cracking,

a pencil point,

 and a T. rex attacking.

Brian J.

I like the stegasaurus
because it has spikes
on its tail.

Carrie

Stegosaurus babies
were hatched from
eggs like reptiles.

CANADA

Wyoming
Utah ★ ★
Colorado ★ ★ Oklahoma

Mexico

Stars show where
Stegosauruses
were found. Toby

A Dinosaur Dig

Fossils show what
the bones were like.
Paleontologists are
the people who like
to dig them out of
the rocks and study them.
Roberto

STICK.

BOOK OF DINOSAUR
FACTS
by Jane

I spy

a fountain,

 a statue on a spool,

and a boy running,

perhaps to school.

I spy

 a log,

a cooking-pot handle,

 a yellow triangle,

and a birthday candle.

= Green
= Orange

ATTERNS
ney match?

Man
Fan
Van
Can
Pan

TODAY'S REBU

2 C U

SLIDE,

I spy

a cave,

 a ball cap to wear,

a school's banner,

 and a polar bear.

I spy

 a race car,

a golden key,

 seven books,

and a big green 3.

I spy

a paintbrush,

a pencil that's blue,

a red pushpin,

and a gold star for you.

I spy 2 matching words.

school bus

ruler

boy running,

perhaps to school

I spy 2 matching words.

pencil that's blue

 bright blue van

polar bear

I spy 3 words that start with the letter S.

seven books

 silver key

school's banner

I spy 2 words that start with the letters SP.

 yellow speedboat

egg that's cracking

 statue on a spool

I spy 3 words that end with the letter G.

ladybug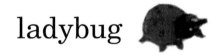

 log

 T. rex attacking

I spy 2 words that end with the letters SH.

shadow fish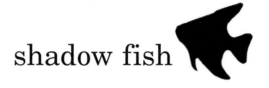

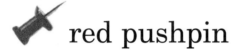 red pushpin

paintbrush

I spy a word and a letter
that rhyme.

R R

 race car

hammer

I spy 2 words that rhyme.

 small red rose

ball cap to wear

 policeman